My Place

Published in Australia by Collins Dove
60-64 Railway Rd, Blackburn, Victoria 3130
(03) 877 1333

Published in Canada by Fitzhenry & Whiteside Limited
195 Allstate Parkway
Markham, Ontario L3R 4T8

ISBN 0 88902 742 0

Illustrated and designed by Donna Rawlins
Typeset in Century by Propaganda Typesetting, Glebe
Colour separations by Colourscan Oversea Pte Ltd
Printed in Singapore

National Library of Australia
Cataloguing-in-Publication data:
Wheatley, Nadia, 1949– .
   My place.
   ISBN 0 85924 575 6
   1. Australia — History — Juvenile fiction. I. Rawlins, Donna, 1956–. II. Title
A823'8

My Place

Nadia Wheatley and Donna Rawlins

The Story of Australia from Now to Then

Fitzhenry & Whiteside
Toronto, Ottowa, Halifax
Winnipeg, Edmonton
Vancouver

1988

My name's Laura and this is my place. I turned ten last week. Our house is the one with the flag on the window. Tony says it shows we're on Aboriginal land, but I think it means the colour of the earth, back home. Mum and Dad live here too, and Terry and Lorraine, and Auntie Bev, and Tony and Diane and their baby Dean. He's my nephew and he's so cute! We come from Bourke, but Dad thought there'd be more jobs in the city.

This is me and Gully. I have to keep her on a lead because she chases cars. She comes from Bourke too. I guess she thinks they're sheep.

This is a map of my place. We've got a McDonalds right on the corner! In the McDonalds yard, there's this big tree, and whenever I sit in it, it always makes me feel good. There's a canal down the bottom of the street, and Mum says it must have been a creek once. It's too dirty to swim in, but Tony made me a tin canoe and now some of the other kids are making them too. If you tip over and go in, the water tastes yucky and your parents go wild.

THEY'RE BULL DOZING IN THE OLD TIP

Church and graveyard

My new School
Cop shop
Cakes Pies
old Furniture
Lebanese takeaway
Post Office
Newspapers
Service Station

Old Junk yard

THE BICENTENNIAL HOTEL

St. V de P OP SHOP
Vietnamese Cafe
Greek deli
Bread shop
Park view restaurant
Thai restaurant
empty
Hamburgers
Dry-cleaner
RAILWAY PUB

STATION

chimneys

FLATS

BIG TREE
McDONALDS
WITH LAWN UNDER IT
LANE
CAR PARK

FLATS

houses

My friend Bianca lives here →

All this colour is houses

MY PLACE → HOME

My friend Soriya lives here

LANE

Vietnamese Grocery

FLATS

FLATS
TRAFFIC LIGHTS

← My friend Tamara lives here

TRUCK YARD

houses

My friend Fatima lives here

LANE

warehouse

CANAL

This road is really busy. Gully isn't allowed up here.

There's a bridge over that way along the canal but I couldn't fit it in. Planes fly that way.

BRICK PITS PARK

It's only just opened this year

TRACK (THERE'S A FENCE WITH LOTS OF GOOD HOLES)

OLD FACTORIES AND STUFF

OLD WOODEN BUILDINGS

For my birthday, Mum said we could have tea at McDonalds! We sat in the outside bit, under the tree, and it felt just like home.

This is my place. I'm Mike. I'm nearly seven. I live with Mum and Dad and Yaya and Auntie Sofia. Yaya's my grandmother, but I call her that because she's Greek. I don't speak very much Greek, but I kind of always understand what she's saying.

We have Easter lunch in the backyard under the grapevine. There's roast lamb and salad, and of course I get chocolate eggs, but we have red real eggs too, and we have a competition about cracking them. I'm the best at it.

This is me and Whiskers. He sneaks in and sleeps on my bed.

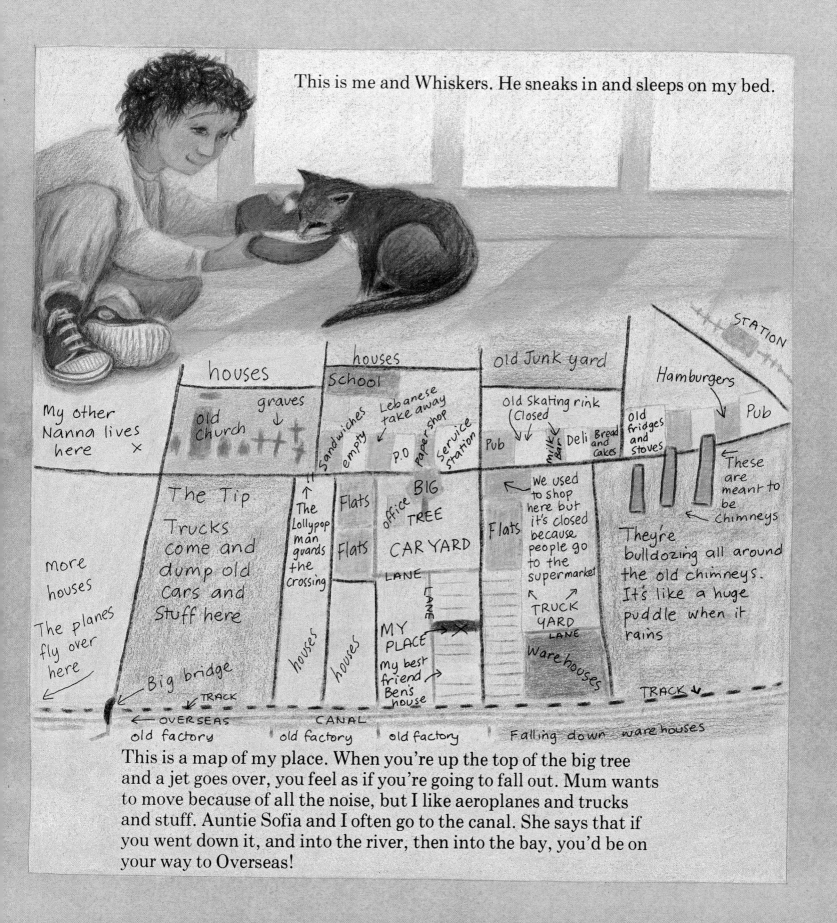

houses

houses

Old Junk yard

STATION

My other Nanna lives here ✗

graves ↓

Old Church

School

Sandwiches

Lebanese take away

empty

P.O

paper shop

Service Station

Old Skating rink (Closed ↓

Milk Bar

Deli

Bread and Cakes

Pub

Hamburgers ↓

Old fridges and stoves

Pub

These are meant to be chimneys

The Tip

Trucks come and dump old Cars and Stuff here

The Lollypop man guards the crossing ↑

Flats

Flats

office

BIG TREE

CAR YARD

LANE

LANE

We used to shop here but it's closed because people go to the supermarket ↖

Flats

TRUCK YARD ↑

LANE

They're bulldozing all around the old chimneys. It's like a huge puddle when it rains

more houses

The planes fly over here ←

houses

houses

MY PLACE

my best friend Ben's house →

Warehouses

Big bridge ←

↓ TRACK

TRACK ↓

← OVERSEAS

old factory

CANAL

old factory

old factory

Falling down warehouses

This is a map of my place. When you're up the top of the big tree and a jet goes over, you feel as if you're going to fall out. Mum wants to move because of all the noise, but I like aeroplanes and trucks and stuff. Auntie Sofia and I often go to the canal. She says that if you went down it, and into the river, then into the bay, you'd be on your way to Overseas!

1968

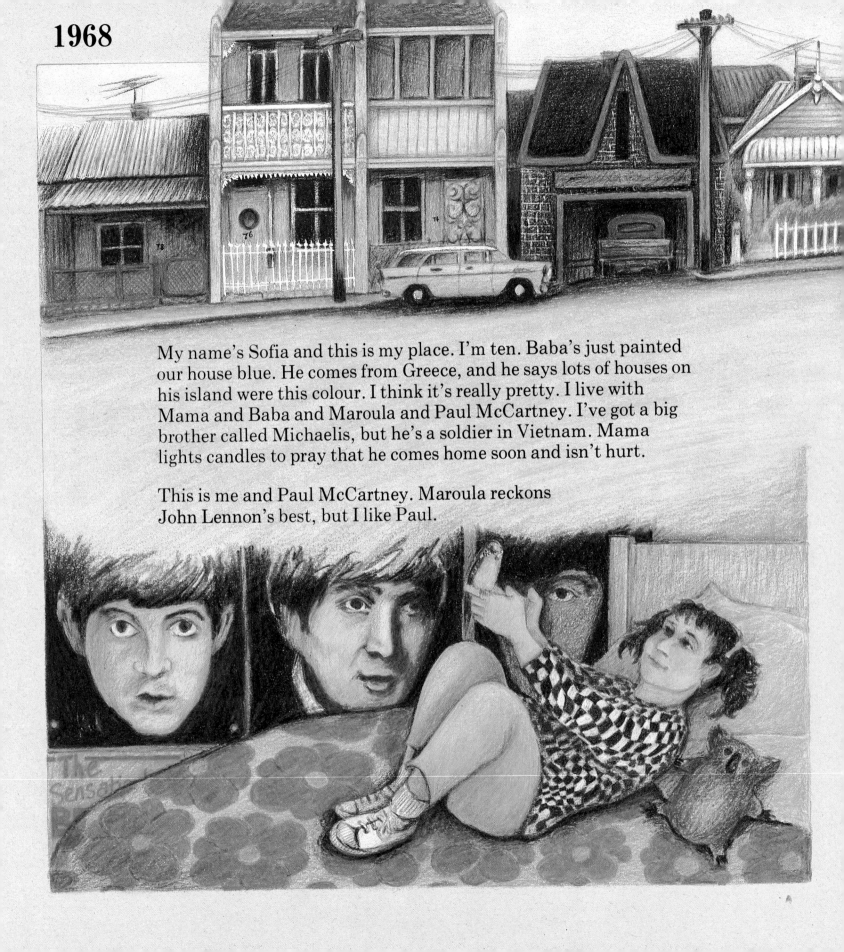

My name's Sofia and this is my place. I'm ten. Baba's just painted our house blue. He comes from Greece, and he says lots of houses on his island were this colour. I think it's really pretty. I live with Mama and Baba and Maroula and Paul McCartney. I've got a big brother called Michaelis, but he's a soldier in Vietnam. Mama lights candles to pray that he comes home soon and isn't hurt.

This is me and Paul McCartney. Maroula reckons John Lennon's best, but I like Paul.

Before Michaelis went away, we had a goodbye party, and he invited a girlfriend! She looked a bit left out because all of us were speaking Greek mostly. Michaelis looked weird in his new haircut. He didn't want to go, but he said the law said he had to. I wish that war would stop.

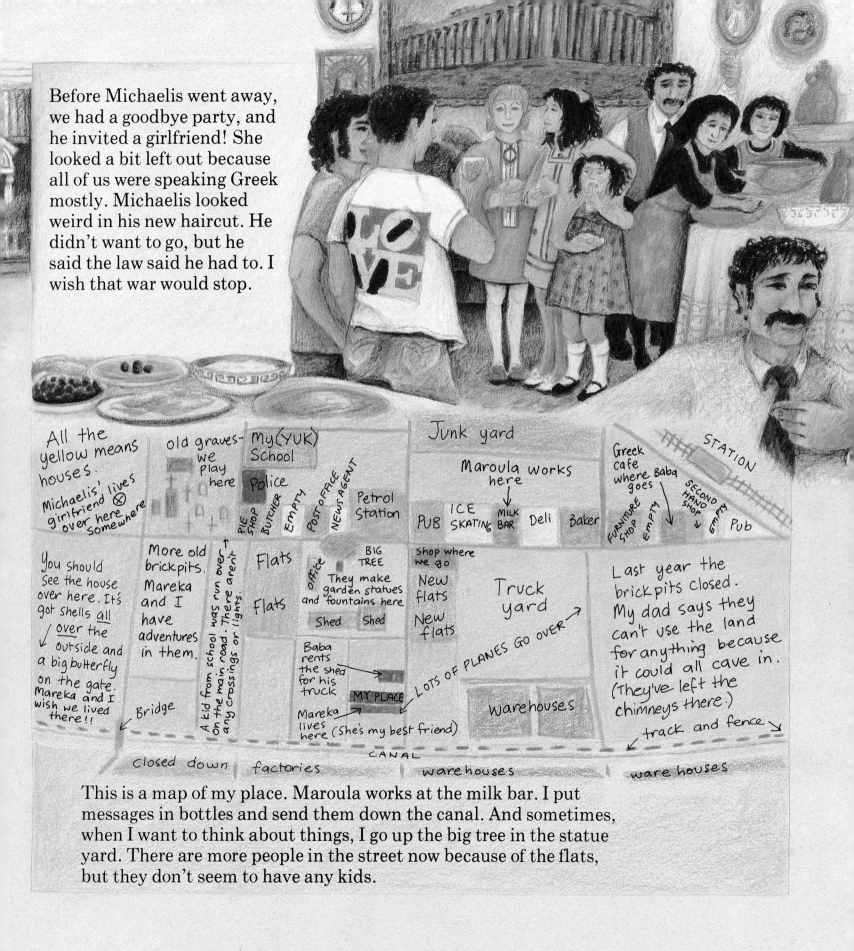

All the yellow means houses.

Michaelis' girlfriend lives over here somewhere ⊗

old graves— we play here

My (YUK) School

Police

Junk yard

Maroula works here

Greek cafe where Baba goes

STATION

PIE SHOP

BUTCHER

EMPTY

POST OFFICE

NEWS AGENT

Petrol Station

PUB

ICE SKATING

MILK BAR

Deli

Baker

FURNITURE SHOP

EMPTY

SECOND HAND SHOP

EMPTY

Pub

You should see the house over here. It's got shells all over the outside and a big butterfly on the gate. Mareka and I wish we lived there!!

Bridge

More old brickpits. Mareka and I have adventures in them.

A kid from school was run over on the main road. There aren't any crossings or lights.

Flats

Flats

Office

BIG TREE

They make garden statues and fountains here

Shed   Shed

Baba rents the shed for his truck →

MY PLACE

Mareka lives here → (She's my best friend)

Shop where we go

New flats

New flats

Truck yard

LOTS OF PLANES GO OVER →

warehouses

Last year the brickpits closed. My dad says they can't use the land for anything because it could all cave in. (They've left the chimneys there.)

← track and fence →

Closed down   factories   CANAL   warehouses   warehouses

This is a map of my place. Maroula works at the milk bar. I put messages in bottles and send them down the canal. And sometimes, when I want to think about things, I go up the big tree in the statue yard. There are more people in the street now because of the flats, but they don't seem to have any kids.

1958

This is my place. My name's Michaelis but at school I say it's Mick. I'm eleven. I was born on Kalymnos but my parents moved here because there wasn't enough work on our island. Baba used to be a sponge diver but now he drives a taxi. Mama sews shirts at home, so she doesn't learn to speak English much. I've already got a sister called Maroula, and now I've got a new one called Sofia. You'd think at least one of them could have been a boy.

After Sofia got christened, we had a party. Baba and I had to make a fence so no one would tread on the new grape vine. Sometimes I think there are more Greek people around here than there are on Kalymnos.

This is a map of my place. Pop and Mrs Malcolm next door have got a television, and sometimes they let me go in and watch it! Up near the depot there's a big tree, and I play Tarzan. That and Zorro are my favourite shows. Sometimes at the end of the day our family goes for a little walk beside the canal, like we used to do around the harbour back on Kalymnos. It's pretty dirty, and there aren't any cafes or anything, but Mama says if you shut your eyes you can pretend it's the Aegean.

This is me and my silkworms. They don't have names. I feed them on mulberry leaves. Their silk is soft and golden.

1948

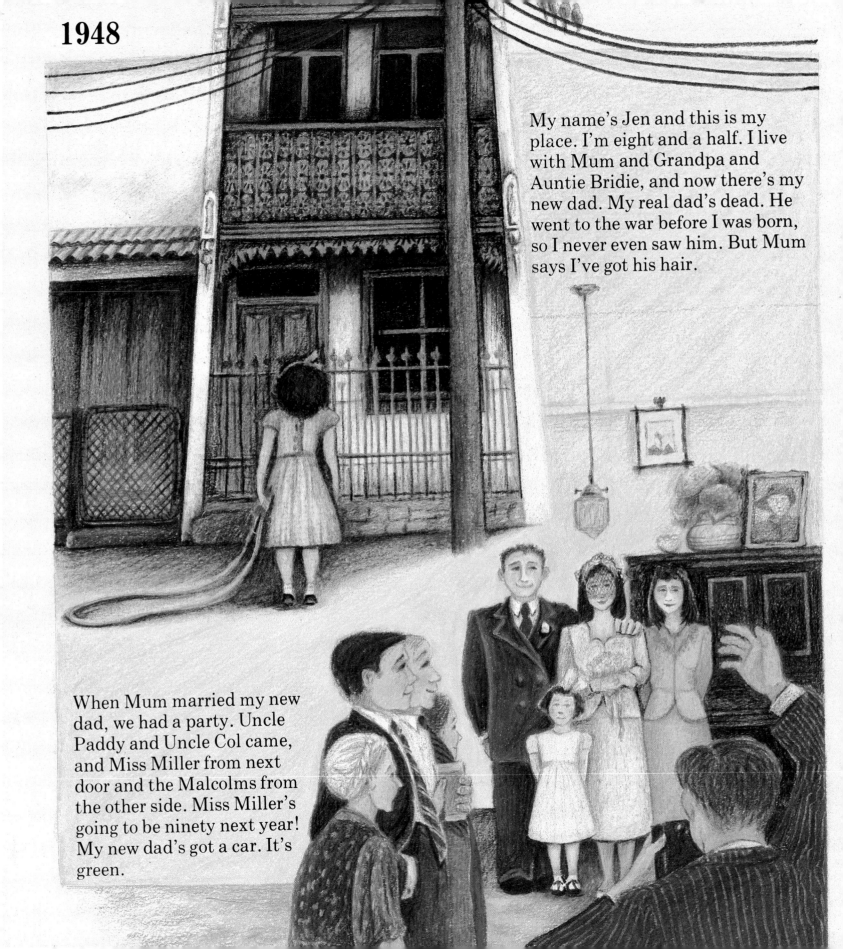

My name's Jen and this is my place. I'm eight and a half. I live with Mum and Grandpa and Auntie Bridie, and now there's my new dad. My real dad's dead. He went to the war before I was born, so I never even saw him. But Mum says I've got his hair.

When Mum married my new dad, we had a party. Uncle Paddy and Uncle Col came, and Miss Miller from next door and the Malcolms from the other side. Miss Miller's going to be ninety next year! My new dad's got a car. It's green.

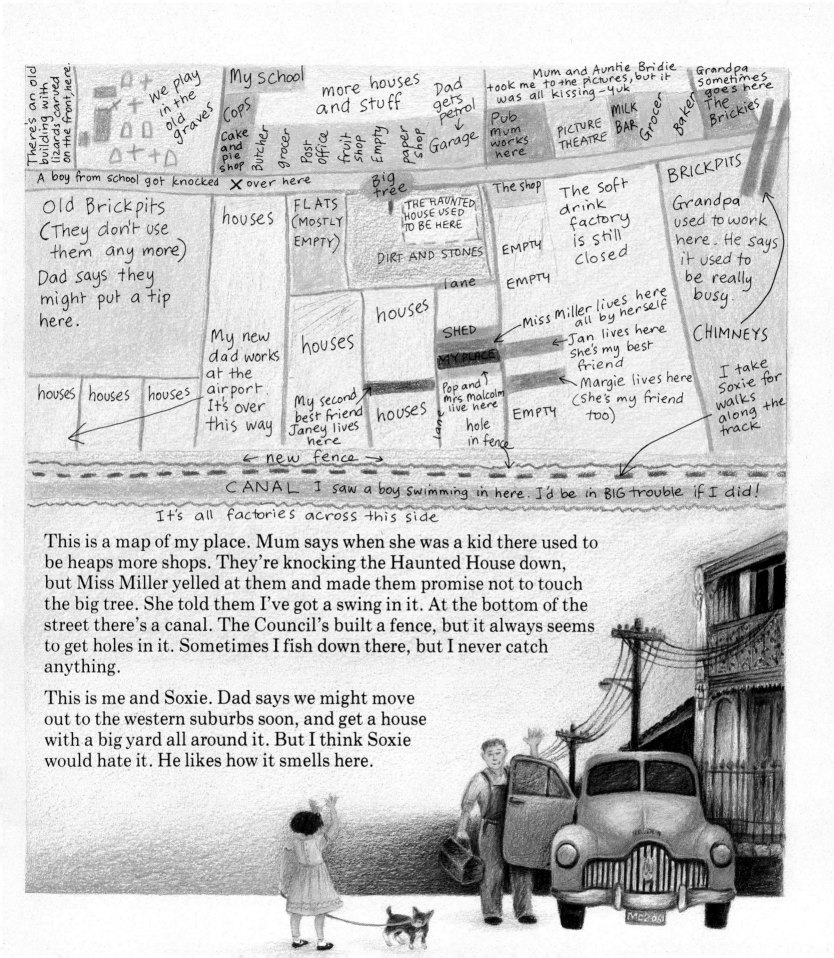

This is a map of my place. Mum says when she was a kid there used to be heaps more shops. They're knocking the Haunted House down, but Miss Miller yelled at them and made them promise not to touch the big tree. She told them I've got a swing in it. At the bottom of the street there's a canal. The Council's built a fence, but it always seems to get holes in it. Sometimes I fish down there, but I never catch anything.

This is me and Soxie. Dad says we might move out to the western suburbs soon, and get a house with a big yard all around it. But I think Soxie would hate it. He likes how it smells here.

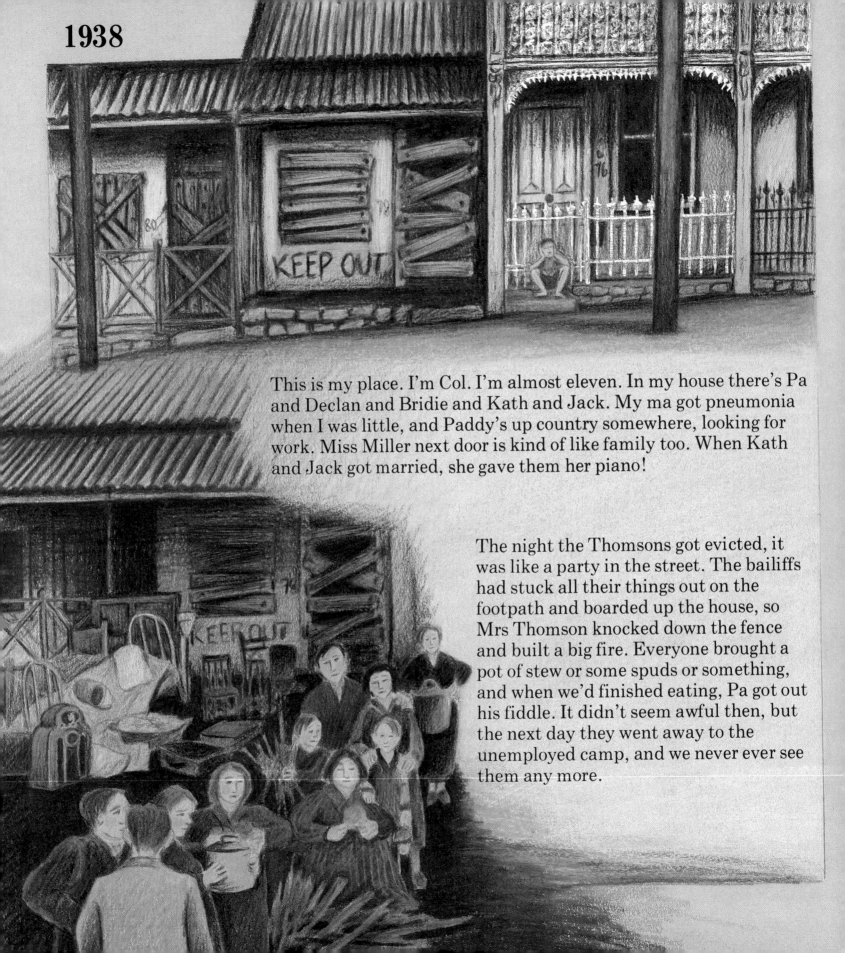

1938

This is my place. I'm Col. I'm almost eleven. In my house there's Pa and Declan and Bridie and Kath and Jack. My ma got pneumonia when I was little, and Paddy's up country somewhere, looking for work. Miss Miller next door is kind of like family too. When Kath and Jack got married, she gave them her piano!

The night the Thomsons got evicted, it was like a party in the street. The bailiffs had stuck all their things out on the footpath and boarded up the house, so Mrs Thomson knocked down the fence and built a big fire. Everyone brought a pot of stew or some spuds or something, and when we'd finished eating, Pa got out his fiddle. It didn't seem awful then, but the next day they went away to the unemployed camp, and we never ever see them any more.

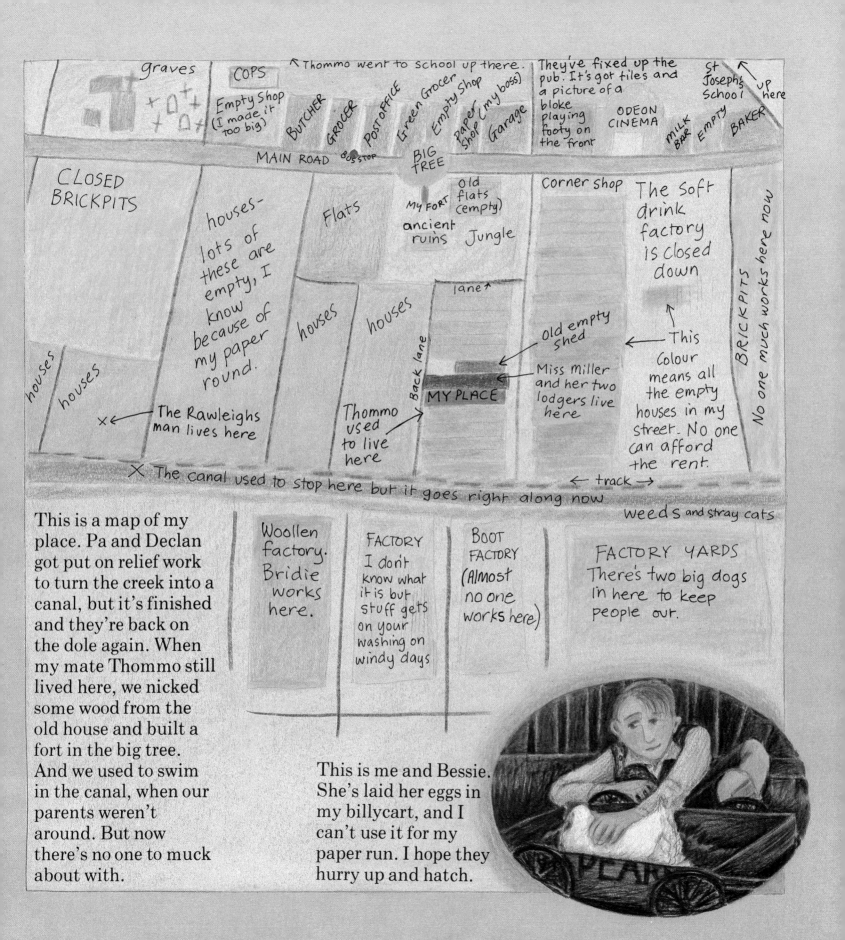

This is a map of my place. Pa and Declan got put on relief work to turn the creek into a canal, but it's finished and they're back on the dole again. When my mate Thommo still lived here, we nicked some wood from the old house and built a fort in the big tree. And we used to swim in the canal, when our parents weren't around. But now there's no one to muck about with.

This is me and Bessie. She's laid her eggs in my billycart, and I can't use it for my paper run. I hope they hurry up and hatch.

1928

My name's Bridie and this is my place. I'm seven. I was born in Dublin, but Pa and Mumma left because there wasn't much work there. Now Pa reckons jobs are getting hard to find here too. The rest of my family is Paddy and Declan and Kathleen and now Colum. Mumma says he was a surprise. Pa and Paddy and Declan all work at the brickworks. Dec had to put his age up because he's only thirteen.

I don't have a pet, but Kath and I look after Col in the afternoon because Mumma cleans at the flats. We put him in the pram and bounce him along the creek track till he goes to sleep. I wish the creek was clean enough to swim in.

This is a map of my place. Last year they put in the poles, so now our lights are electric! It's really exciting living here because the aerodrome's just nearby, and sometimes aeroplanes fly over. I climb up the big tree and wave to the pilots. Mumma says we're lucky here because we've got good neighbours. Miss Miller lets Kath and me play her piano, and if we catch Henry's bus he won't let us pay. The Thomsons on the other side have got a wireless! Lorna Thomson's my best friend.

We had a party last Saint Patrick's Day. He's the Saint of Ireland, and we all wear green for him and sing and dance. Pa got a bit sad because he was missing home, so Mumma invited the Next Doors in to cheer him up.

OLD GRAVE-YARD. LORNA AND I PLAY SPOOKS HERE

SOME KIDS GO TO SCHOOL HERE BUT WE GO TO ST JOSEPHS

Henry used to own the garage but now he's got the bus.

HOUSES

Centennial Hotel. Henry goes here

WE GO TO SCHOOL UP THIS WAY

This is the pub where Pa goes

HOUSES

COPS

HOUSES

we go to the Saturday matinee

BRICKIES ARMS

SHOPS

BAKER BUTCHER GROCER P.O. GREEN GROCER CHINESE GROCER PAPER SHOP

PICTURE THEATRE MILK BAR LOLLY SHOP BAKER

They only just missed the tree

They're just making the road wider

BIG TREE

Red spots means Henry's bus stops here

New block of flats

BIG HOUSE is flats now Mumma cleans them

New corner shop

They knocked shops down for the road

MORE BRICKPITS

New block of flats

Jungley bushes

* Shepherd's Soft drink factory. YUM YUM (Mumma reckons it's bad for you!)

TALL CHIMNEYS - HOW COME THE PLANES DON'T BUMP INTO THEM?

Brickpits where my Father and my brothers work

HOUSES

falling down shed

LANE

HOUSES

The aerodrome is over this way Somewhere

Roy, the Bottle-o has a shed over there

LANE

MY PLACE

Henry keeps his bus here Miss Miller and Henry's

Lorna Thomson lives here

WOOPS, A BIT MESSY

CANAL

THIS BRIDGE IS A BIT FURTHER DOWN
TRACK WHERE WE GO ALONG

WEEDS AND JUNK

CREEK

FACTORY FACTORY FACTORY

FACTORIES AND OTHER STUFF LIKE THAT

1918

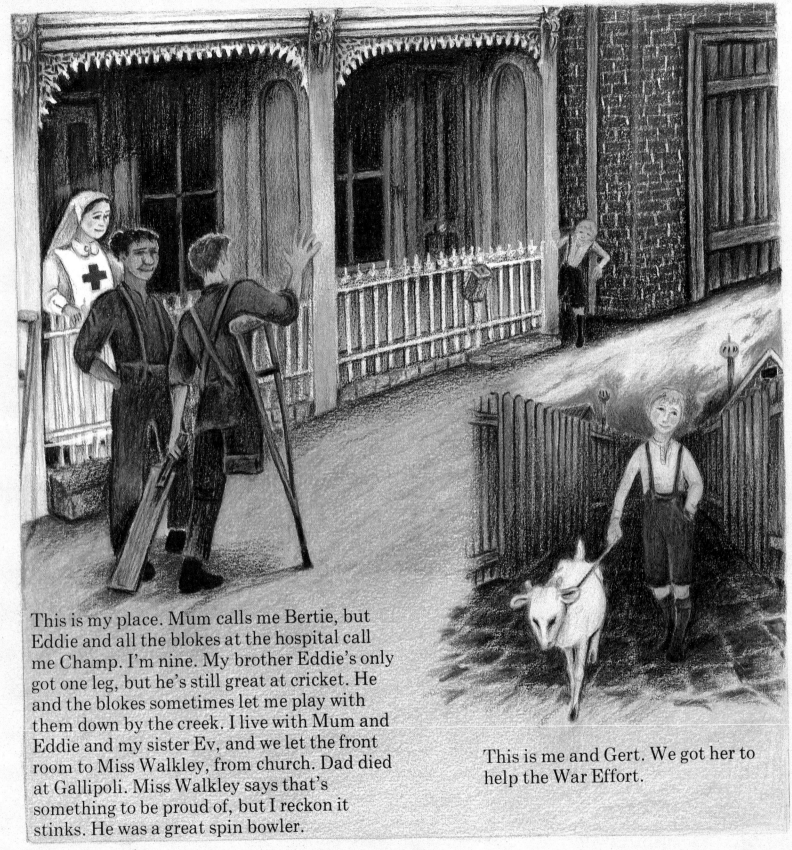

This is my place. Mum calls me Bertie, but Eddie and all the blokes at the hospital call me Champ. I'm nine. My brother Eddie's only got one leg, but he's still great at cricket. He and the blokes sometimes let me play with them down by the creek. I live with Mum and Eddie and my sister Ev, and we let the front room to Miss Walkley, from church. Dad died at Gallipoli. Miss Walkley says that's something to be proud of, but I reckon it stinks. He was a great spin bowler.

This is me and Gert. We got her to help the War Effort.

This is a map of my place. Mum works in the kitchen at the hospital, and when Ev comes home from the factory she puts on her VAD dress and goes over there too. I've got a treehouse in the big tree. Mum says we might have to move to the country because we can't afford to live here now, but I don't want to.

This place used to make headstones

HOUSES

Miss Walkley plays the organ.

OUR CHURCH

SCHOOL

POLICE

(I think this one is the post office) P.O

THE BRICKPITS HERE ARE CLOSED NOW

Mr Miller's shop and petrol pumps
CENTENNIAL HOTEL

Shops

LOTS OF TRAINS

BRICKMAKERS ARMS HOTEL

These dots mean electric light poles

BRICKPITS

LOTS OF TRAFFIC

BIG TREE

SQUISHY FIGS

HOSPITAL
CHAIRS AND STUFF FOR THE OLD SHEDS SOLDIERS

Shops

RAILWAY VIEW HOTEL

X

CORDIAL FACTORY

BRICKPITS WITH THE BIGGEST CHIMNEYS

BRICKPITS

LANE

We had our party here when the war ended

HOUSES

HOUSES

Eddie's best mate, Sid, (from the army) lives here

HOUSES

LANE

HOUSES

HOUSES

Old shed
Miller's house
MY PLACE

The girl who lives on top of this shop has got a rabbit in a box. Eddie reckons it's safer in the box. He reckons if she lets it out it might end up someone's dinner!

ICE WORKS

CANAL

HOUSES

X

X

WE PLAY CRICKET HERE

TRACK

FACTORY BRIDGE

FACTORY

WOOLLEN FACTORY

WOOLLEN FACTORY

IRON FOUNDRY

BOOT FACTORY WHERE EV MAKES SOLDIERS' BOOTS

I GRAZE GERT ON THE WEEDS BESIDE THE TRACK

On the day the war ended, people danced in the street and blokes hugged each other on the lawn. But Mum started crying. Then Miss Miller cried, then Mr Miller even cried, because their Tom and Fred won't be coming home either. So I did some stilt-walking on Eddie's crutches and made them stop.

1908

My name's Evelyn and this is my place. I'm ten. We moved here because it's close to the city for Father to get to the bank. Mother teaches music at the college, but of course Eddie and I go to the ordinary school. On the way home, we always wait near the petrol pump on Müllers' corner in case a motor car stops. Father says the main road will be tar soon, and there'll be even more traffic. Of course, Eddie pesters Father about when will we get a motor car, but you'd have to be as rich as anything for that.

This is me and Old Ned. He used to pull a horse bus but Mr Müller put him out to pasture when the trams went electric. He says poor Ned just couldn't keep up.

Last Cracker Night all our street had a bonfire down near the creek. We got crackers from the Chinese shop. Mr Müller said it reminded him of old times.

This is a map of my place. On weekends I play caves under the big tree. Mr Müller says, when he was a boy, a dragon lived across the creek. When I was little I used to believe him.

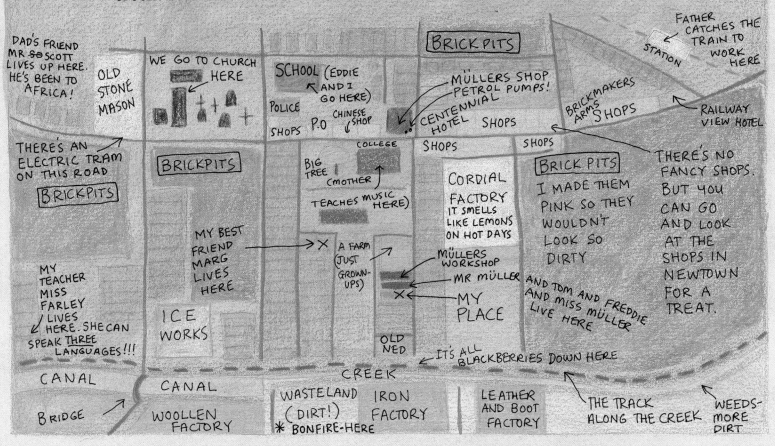

1898

This is my place. My name's Rowley. I'm eight. My mum and me, we rent the upstairs front room. Auntie Adie's got the middle room and Miss Singer's got the back. Mum works at the laundry with Auntie Adie. She's not really my auntie, but I call her that. Downstairs, there's Mr Merry. He does photographs, but on weekends he has an icecream cart, and he lets me and Tommy Müller help him. Tom lives next door. His auntie's got a bicycle!

This is a map of my place. The big tree belongs to the posh school, but I climb it anyway. A bit down the creek, it turns into a canal, and there are barges. Before my dad went away, he helped build it. Mum says he just couldn't find any more work, and one day he might come back.

76

STATION

RAILWAY LINE

MORE BRICKPITS

You catch mr Müller's horse bus here

SCHOOL

POLICE

Chinese shop MÜLLERS

P.O.

Centennial Hotel. Tommy and me get mr merry's beer here.

Brickmakers Arms

RAILWAY VIEW HOTEL

Archie reckons there's ghosts here.

BRICKPITS

There's tracks for the steam tram on this road

The kid here got gastro

All these shops are empty

This is the laundry where Mum and Auntie Adie work.

BIG TREE

POSH SCHOOL

POSH KIDS KEEP THEIR CRICKET AND FOOTBALL STUFF HERE

There's a farm I forgot

BRICKPITS

My dad used to work here but he got a bad cough and the boss told him to leave.

Archie lives here. He's a bully. He picks on me if I walk down this street!

BRICKPITS

BRICKPITS

There's some houses here they never finished

Iceworks

The cows for the dairy live here

Müllers workshop.

My mate Tom Müller lives here with his Mum and dad and Freddie and their Auntie

My PLACE!

Ned Kelly grazes here

MORE BRICKPITS

CREEK TRACK

CREEK TRACK

CANAL - Dad built this

All weeds and rubbish

Bridge

They're building a new factory here. Maybe my dad can get a job here.

Some sort of ironworks

Vegetable garden

new road

All this is weeds, but sometimes pumpkin comes up all by itself. Yuk, I hate pumpkin.

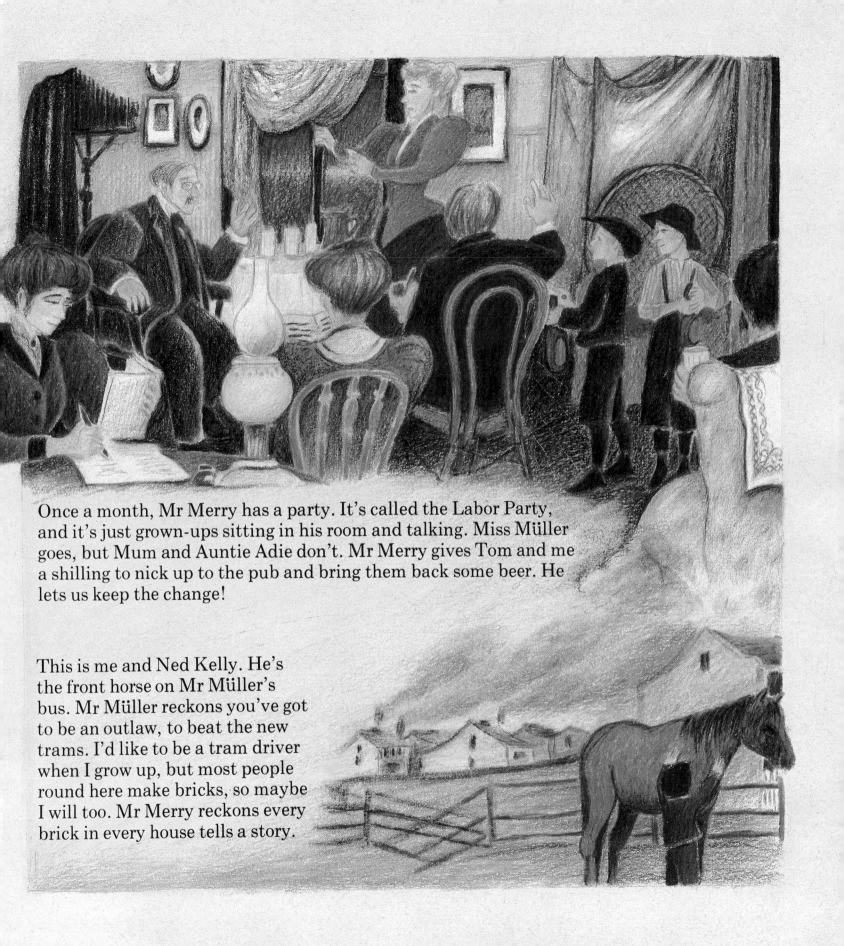

Once a month, Mr Merry has a party. It's called the Labor Party, and it's just grown-ups sitting in his room and talking. Miss Müller goes, but Mum and Auntie Adie don't. Mr Merry gives Tom and me a shilling to nick up to the pub and bring them back some beer. He lets us keep the change!

This is me and Ned Kelly. He's the front horse on Mr Müller's bus. Mr Müller reckons you've got to be an outlaw, to beat the new trams. I'd like to be a tram driver when I grow up, but most people round here make bricks, so maybe I will too. Mr Merry reckons every brick in every house tells a story.

1888

My name's Victoria and this is my place. I'm nearly eleven. My father is a builder and he built our house, and Father and Mother and Wesley and Charles and May and I are the first people ever ever to live here! Father built the next door house too, for the Müllers, and now he's started two more houses on the other side. Our house is the biggest. We've got three bedrooms upstairs, and downstairs there's a parlour and a dining-room, then the breezeway, then the kitchen. We've even got tap water. Mother says it's like a Dream Come True, but sometimes Father looks worried.

This is a map of my place. Mother reckons you get sick if you even look at the creek, but Father says it'll get better soon when they finish making the sewerage. Sometimes I play on the swing in the big tree, but the Owen girls don't talk to me. As if I'd care! The hotel's just changed its name because of the Centenary. Mother won't even let me walk on that side of the road. We're all in the Temperance League.

THIS IS A CHURCH BUT WE DON'T GO HERE

STONE MASON

SCHOOL

POLICE

CHEMIST

BAKER

GROCER

POST OFFICE

DRAPER

CHINESE SHOP

BOOKS

THE MÜLLERS SHOP

← OUR CHURCH IS UP THIS WAY

RAILWAY LINE

RAILWAY STATION X

CENTENNIAL HOTEL

BLACKSMITH

BAKER

BUTCHER

FRUITSHOP

STATION HOTEL

GROCER AND OTHER HOTEL

SHOPS

BIG HOUSE

BRICKPITS

DAIRY

HOUSES

BIG TREE

OWEN'S HOUSE

STABLES

THIS IS WHERE YOU CATCH THE MÜLLERS HORSE BUS

BRICKPITS—LOTS OF CHIMNEYS AND SMOKE

TEMPERANCE HALL (THERE'S A CLUB FOR GIRLS HERE, YOU SEW AND SING HYMNS & STUFF)

HOUSES

BRICKPITS

OWEN'S HORSE PADDOCK

There's a farm here

← MÜLLER'S WORKSHOP
← MÜLLER'S HOUSE
← OUR HOUSE
← FATHER IS BUILDING THESE HOUSES

→ THIS IS OUR BACK LANE THE NIGHT CART GOES DOWN THERE

MR MÜLLER'S HORSE IS HERE

ALL THE GREY BITS ARE HOUSES   TRACK →   LECK'S VEGETABLES   ↖ CREEK

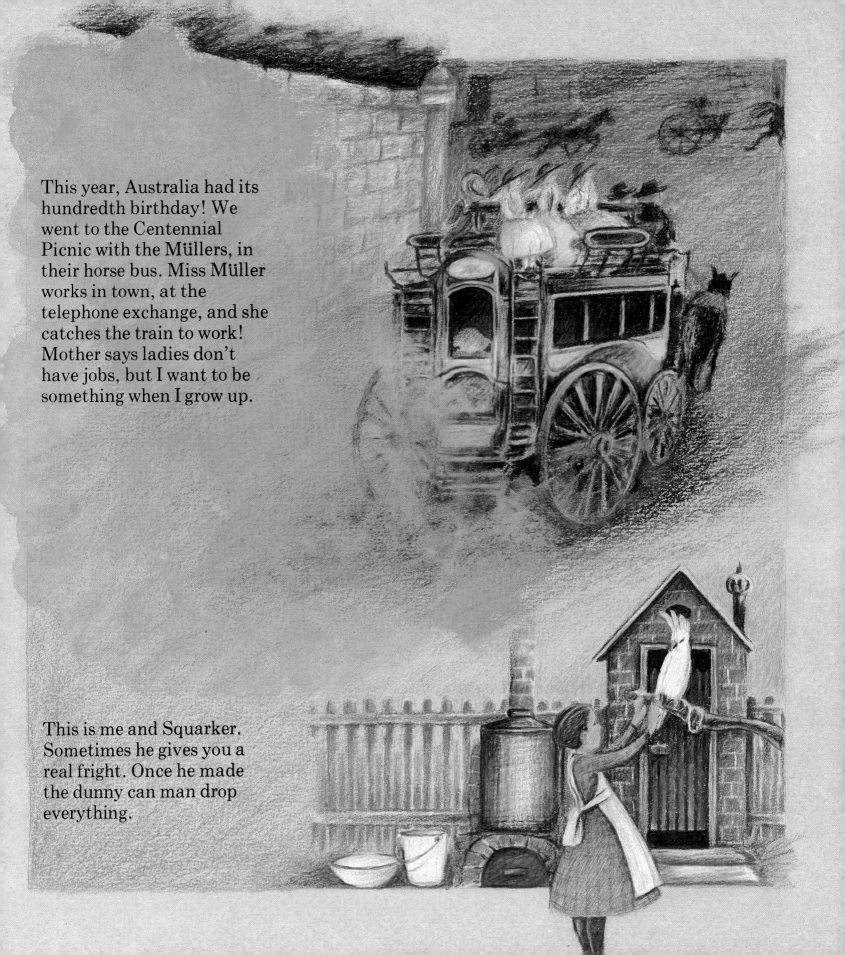

This year, Australia had its hundredth birthday! We went to the Centennial Picnic with the Müllers, in their horse bus. Miss Müller works in town, at the telephone exchange, and she catches the train to work! Mother says ladies don't have jobs, but I want to be something when I grow up.

This is me and Squarker. Sometimes he gives you a real fright. Once he made the dunny can man drop everything.

1878

This is my place. My name's really Heinrich, but everyone except my grandparents calls me Henry. I'm ten. When my mother died, Minna stopped being a teacher, and she looks after Father and Anna and me. I used to have a little brother too, but he got the gastro. My grandparents and Uncle Wolf live on top of the new shop. My grandfather says that one day I will own it, but I want to be a balloonist.
I didn't tell him that.

MÜLLER & SONS

This is me and Gretchen. She's Minna's cat, but she's mine too.

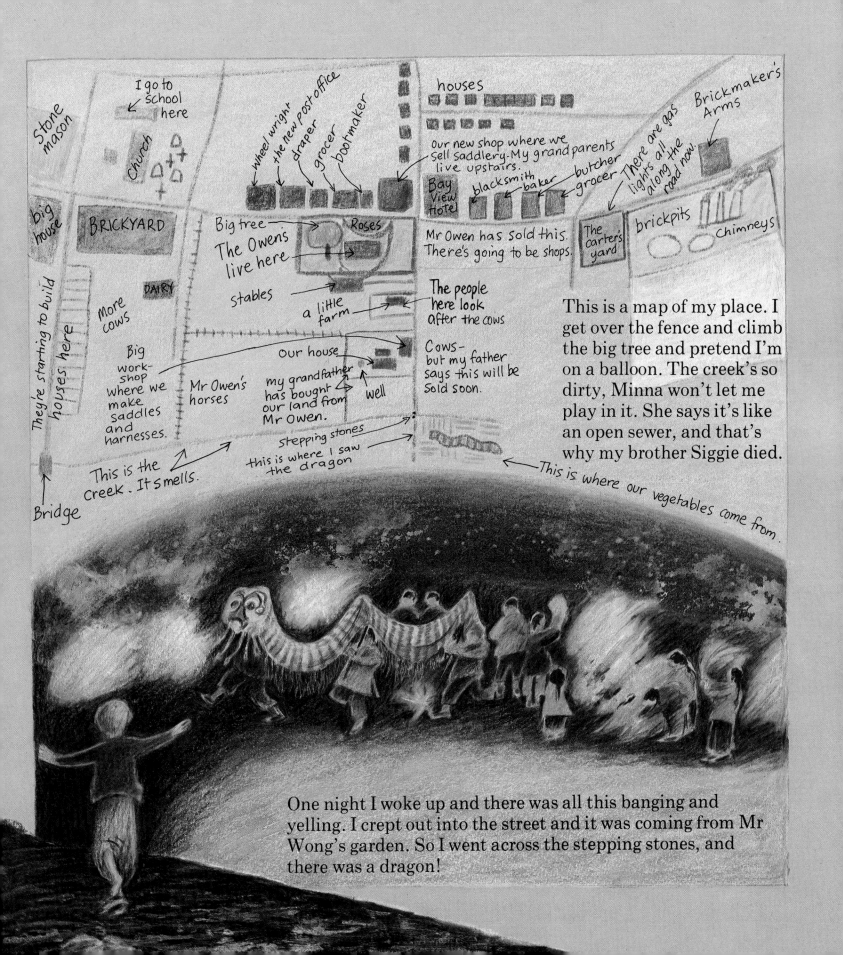

Stone mason

I go to school here

Church

big house

BRICKYARD

They're starting to build houses here

More cows

DAIRY

Big work-shop where we make saddles and harnesses.

Mr Owen's horses

Bridge

This is the creek. It smells.

stepping stones
this is where I saw the dragon

my grandfather has bought our land from Mr Owen.

Our house

Well

wheelwright
the new post office
draper
grocer
bootmaker

Big tree
The Owens live here
Roses
Stables
a little farm

Our new shop where we sell saddlery. My grandparents live upstairs.

Bay View Hotel

houses

blacksmith
baker
butcher
grocer

There are gas lights all along the road now.

Brickmaker's Arms

Mr Owen has sold this. There's going to be shops.

The people here look after the cows

Cows — but my father says this will be sold soon.

The carter's yard

brickpits

Chimneys

This is where our vegetables come from.

This is a map of my place. I get over the fence and climb the big tree and pretend I'm on a balloon. The creek's so dirty, Minna won't let me play in it. She says it's like an open sewer, and that's why my brother Siggie died.

One night I woke up and there was all this banging and yelling. I crept out into the street and it was coming from Mr Wong's garden. So I went across the stepping stones, and there was a dragon!

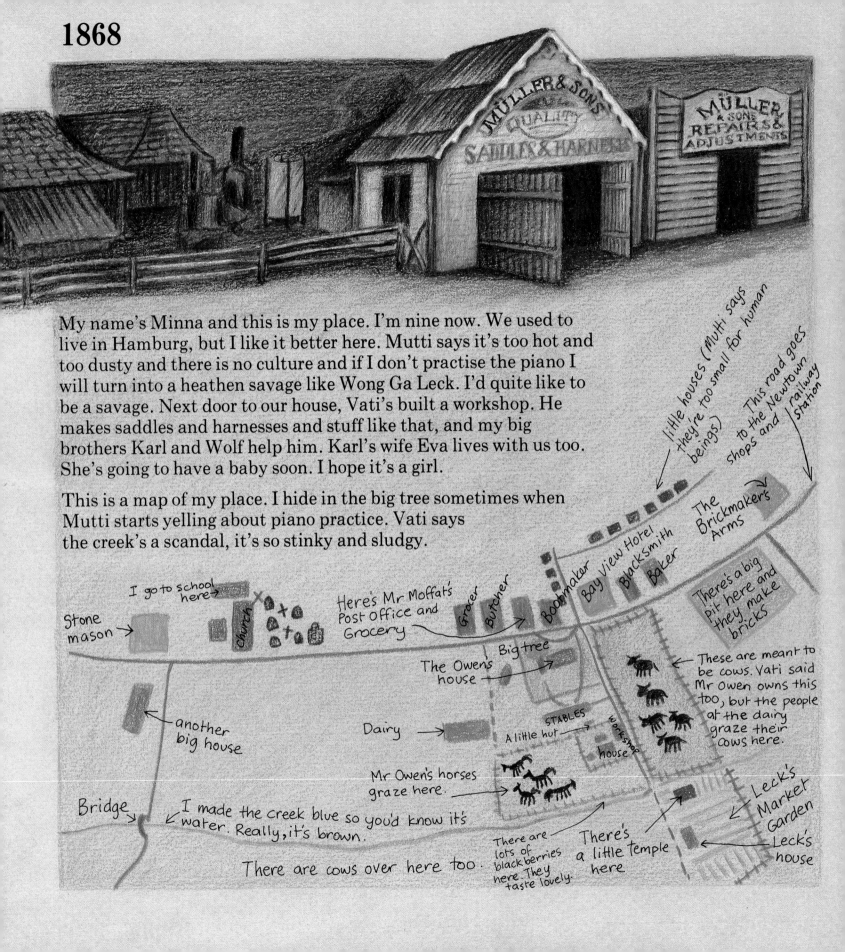

My name's Minna and this is my place. I'm nine now. We used to live in Hamburg, but I like it better here. Mutti says it's too hot and too dusty and there is no culture and if I don't practise the piano I will turn into a heathen savage like Wong Ga Leck. I'd quite like to be a savage. Next door to our house, Vati's built a workshop. He makes saddles and harnesses and stuff like that, and my big brothers Karl and Wolf help him. Karl's wife Eva lives with us too. She's going to have a baby soon. I hope it's a girl.

This is a map of my place. I hide in the big tree sometimes when Mutti starts yelling about piano practice. Vati says the creek's a scandal, it's so stinky and sludgy.

MÜLLER & SONS
QUALITY
SADDLERY & HARNESS

MÜLLER & SONS REPAIRS & ADJUSTMENTS

little houses (Mutti says they're too small for human beings)

This road goes to the Newtown shops and railway station

The Brickmaker's Arms

Boatmaker
Bay View Hotel
Blacksmith
Baker

There's a big Pit here and they make bricks

I go to school here →

Here's Mr Moffat's Post Office and Grocery

Grocer
Butcher

Stone mason →

Church

These are meant to be cows. Vati said Mr Owen owns this too, but the people at the dairy graze their cows here.

The Owen's house →

Big tree

another big house

Dairy →

STABLES
A little hut →
Workshop house

Leck's Market Garden

Mr Owen's horses graze here. →

Bridge →

I made the creek blue so you'd know it's water. Really, it's brown.

There are cows over here too.

There are lots of blackberries here. They taste lovely.

There's a little temple here

Leck's house

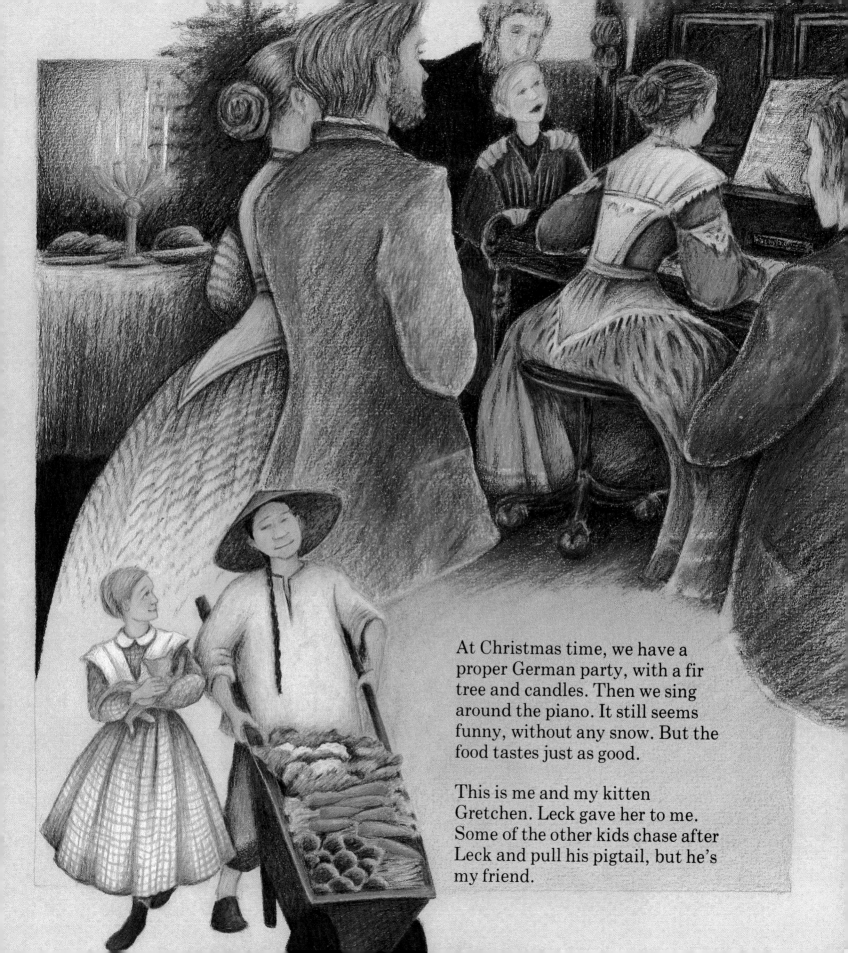

At Christmas time, we have a proper German party, with a fir tree and candles. Then we sing around the piano. It still seems funny, without any snow. But the food tastes just as good.

This is me and my kitten Gretchen. Leck gave her to me. Some of the other kids chase after Leck and pull his pigtail, but he's my friend.

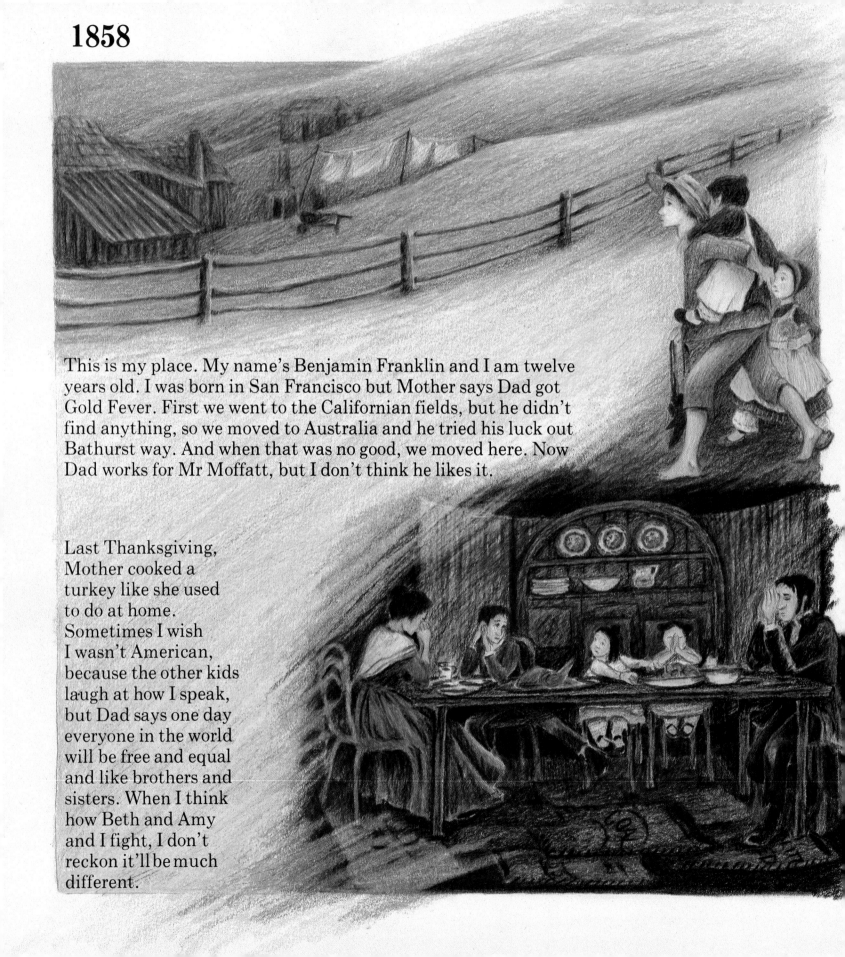

1858

This is my place. My name's Benjamin Franklin and I am twelve years old. I was born in San Francisco but Mother says Dad got Gold Fever. First we went to the Californian fields, but he didn't find anything, so we moved to Australia and he tried his luck out Bathurst way. And when that was no good, we moved here. Now Dad works for Mr Moffatt, but I don't think he likes it.

Last Thanksgiving, Mother cooked a turkey like she used to do at home. Sometimes I wish I wasn't American, because the other kids laugh at how I speak, but Dad says one day everyone in the world will be free and equal and like brothers and sisters. When I think how Beth and Amy and I fight, I don't reckon it'll be much different.

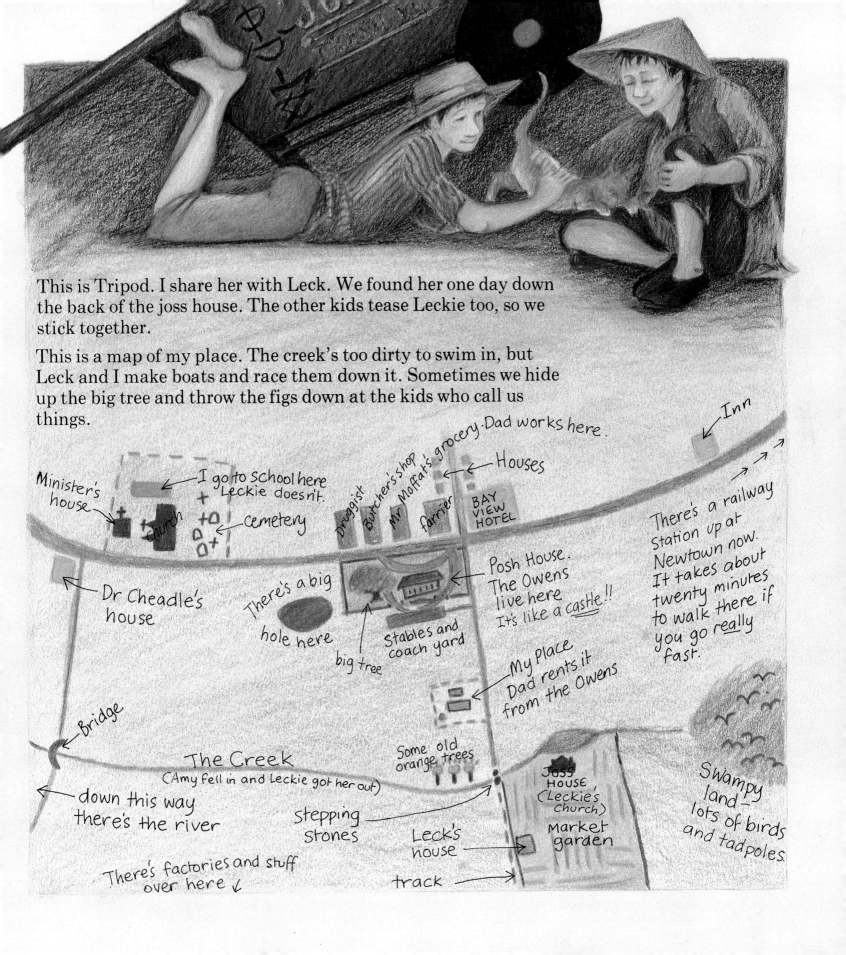

This is Tripod. I share her with Leck. We found her one day down the back of the joss house. The other kids tease Leckie too, so we stick together.

This is a map of my place. The creek's too dirty to swim in, but Leck and I make boats and race them down it. Sometimes we hide up the big tree and throw the figs down at the kids who call us things.

Inn

Dad works here.

Mr Moffat's grocery

Butcher's shop

Druggist

Houses

I go to school here Leckie doesn't.

Minister's house

church

cemetery

farrier

BAY VIEW HOTEL

There's a railway station up at Newtown now. It takes about twenty minutes to walk there if you go really fast.

Dr Cheadle's house

There's a big

hole here

big tree

Posh House. The Owens live here It's like a castle!!

Stables and coach yard

My Place Dad rents it from the Owens

Bridge

The Creek (Amy fell in and Leckie got her out)

Some old orange trees

Swampy land - lots of birds and tadpoles.

down this way there's the river

stepping stones

Joss HOUSE, (Leckie's church)

market garden

Leck's house

There's factories and stuff over here ↓

track

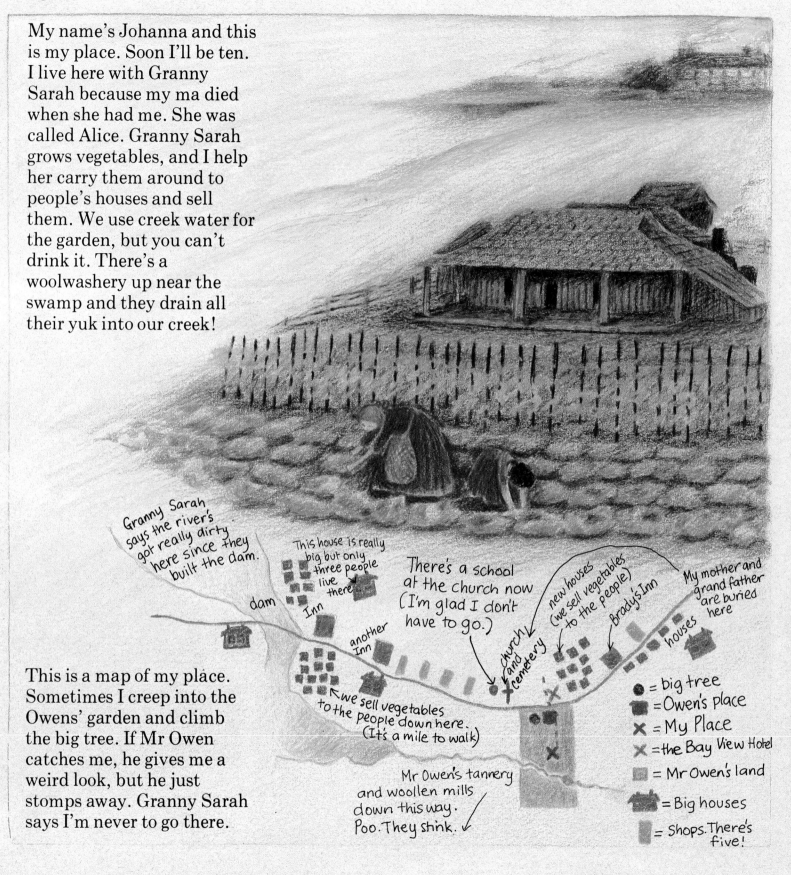

My name's Johanna and this is my place. Soon I'll be ten. I live here with Granny Sarah because my ma died when she had me. She was called Alice. Granny Sarah grows vegetables, and I help her carry them around to people's houses and sell them. We use creek water for the garden, but you can't drink it. There's a woolwashery up near the swamp and they drain all their yuk into our creek!

This is a map of my place. Sometimes I creep into the Owens' garden and climb the big tree. If Mr Owen catches me, he gives me a weird look, but he just stomps away. Granny Sarah says I'm never to go there.

Granny Sarah says the river's got really dirty here since they built the dam.

This house is really big but only three people live there.

dam

Inn

another Inn

we sell vegetables to the people down here. (It's a mile to walk)

There's a school at the church now (I'm glad I don't have to go.)

church and cemetery

new houses (we sell vegetables to the people)

Brady's Inn

My mother and grandfather are buried here

houses

Mr Owen's tannery and woollen mills down this way. Poo. They stink.

● = big tree
■ = Owen's place
✗ = My Place
✕ = the Bay View Hotel
▪ = Mr Owen's land
🏠 = Big houses
▪ = Shops. There's five!

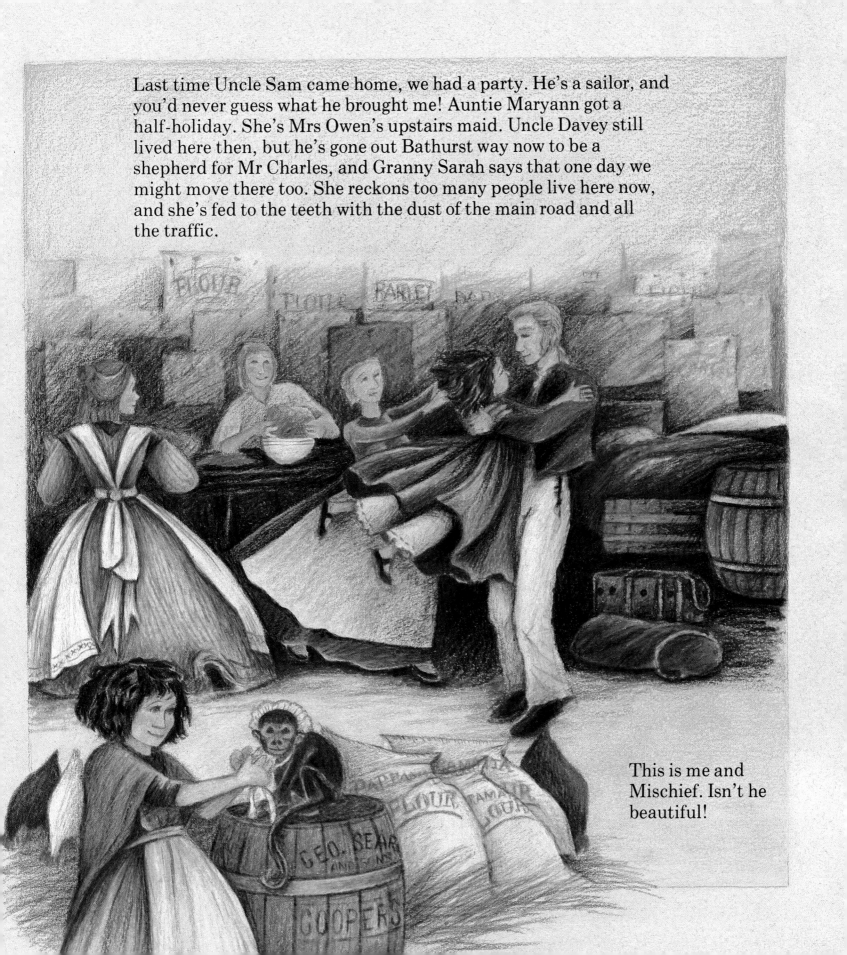

Last time Uncle Sam came home, we had a party. He's a sailor, and you'd never guess what he brought me! Auntie Maryann got a half-holiday. She's Mrs Owen's upstairs maid. Uncle Davey still lived here then, but he's gone out Bathurst way now to be a shepherd for Mr Charles, and Granny Sarah says that one day we might move there too. She reckons too many people live here now, and she's fed to the teeth with the dust of the main road and all the traffic.

This is me and Mischief. Isn't he beautiful!

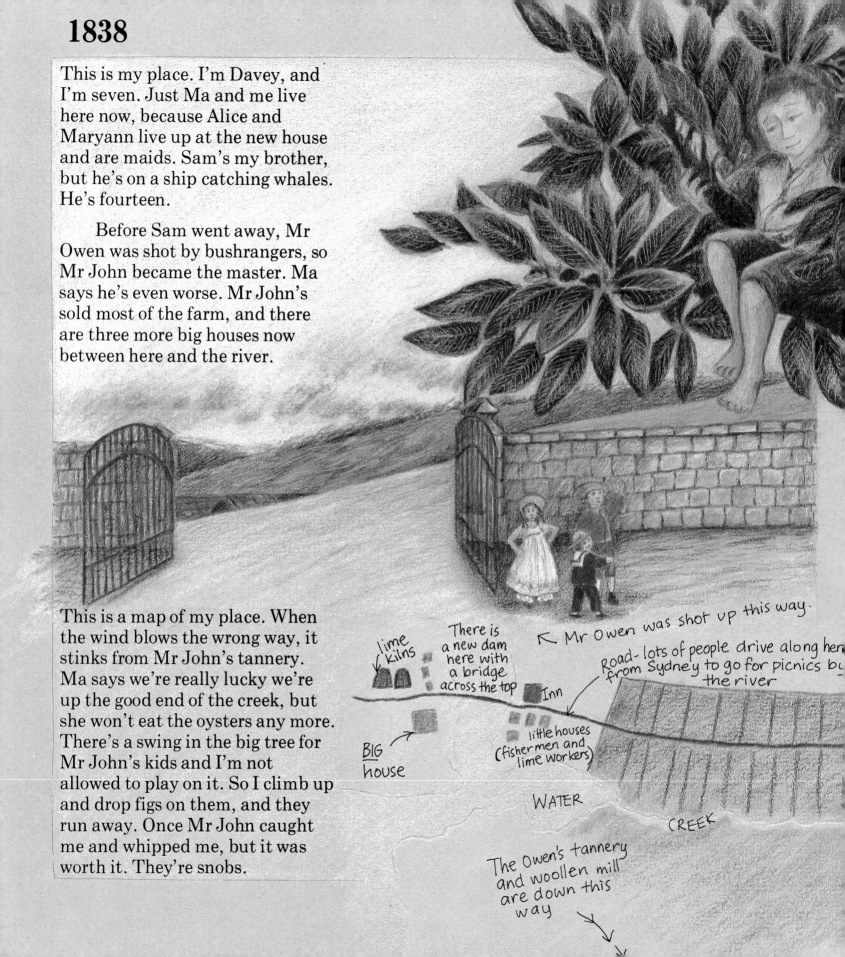

1838

This is my place. I'm Davey, and I'm seven. Just Ma and me live here now, because Alice and Maryann live up at the new house and are maids. Sam's my brother, but he's on a ship catching whales. He's fourteen.

Before Sam went away, Mr Owen was shot by bushrangers, so Mr John became the master. Ma says he's even worse. Mr John's sold most of the farm, and there are three more big houses now between here and the river.

This is a map of my place. When the wind blows the wrong way, it stinks from Mr John's tannery. Ma says we're really lucky we're up the good end of the creek, but she won't eat the oysters any more. There's a swing in the big tree for Mr John's kids and I'm not allowed to play on it. So I climb up and drop figs on them, and they run away. Once Mr John caught me and whipped me, but it was worth it. They're snobs.

lime kilns

There is a new dam here with a bridge across the top

Inn

← Mr Owen was shot up this way.

Road- lots of people drive along here from Sydney to go for picnics by the river

BIG house

little houses (fishermen and lime workers)

WATER

CREEK

The Owen's tannery and woollen mill are down this way

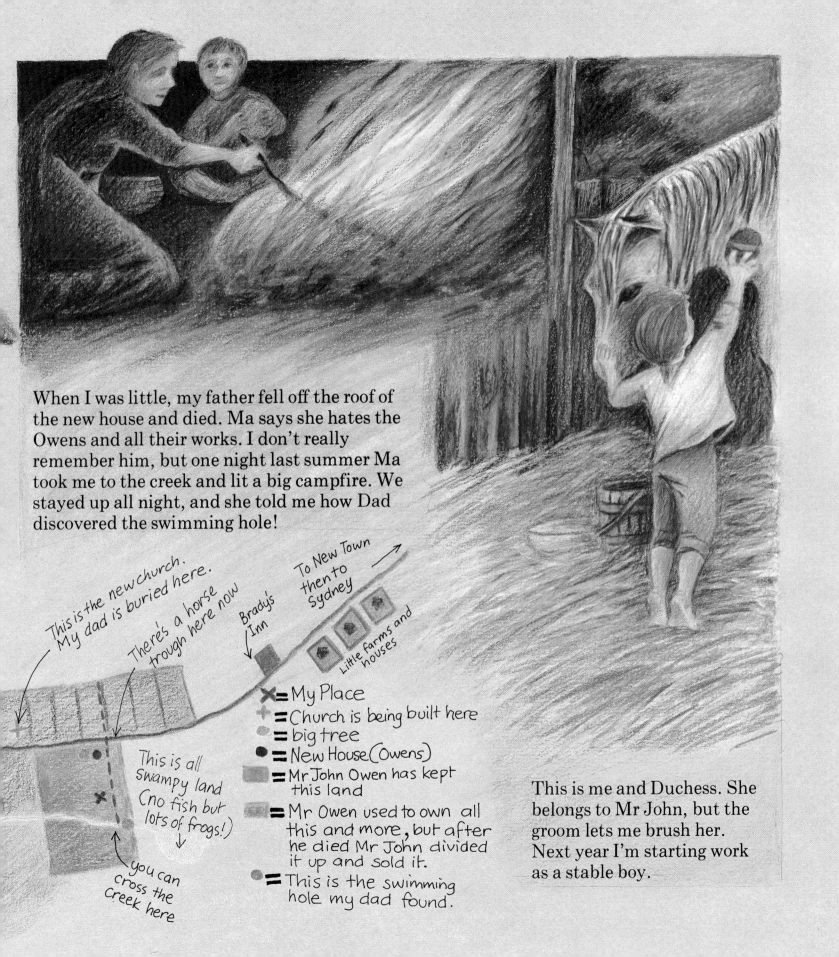

When I was little, my father fell off the roof of the new house and died. Ma says she hates the Owens and all their works. I don't really remember him, but one night last summer Ma took me to the creek and lit a big campfire. We stayed up all night, and she told me how Dad discovered the swimming hole!

This is the new church. My dad is buried here.

There's a horse trough here now

Brady's Inn

To New Town then to Sydney

Little farms and houses

This is all swampy land (no fish but lots of frogs!)

you can cross the creek here

X = My Place

✚ = Church is being built here

= big tree

● = New House (Owens)

= Mr John Owen has kept this land

= Mr Owen used to own all this and more, but after he died Mr John divided it up and sold it.

= This is the swimming hole my dad found.

This is me and Duchess. She belongs to Mr John, but the groom lets me brush her. Next year I'm starting work as a stable boy.

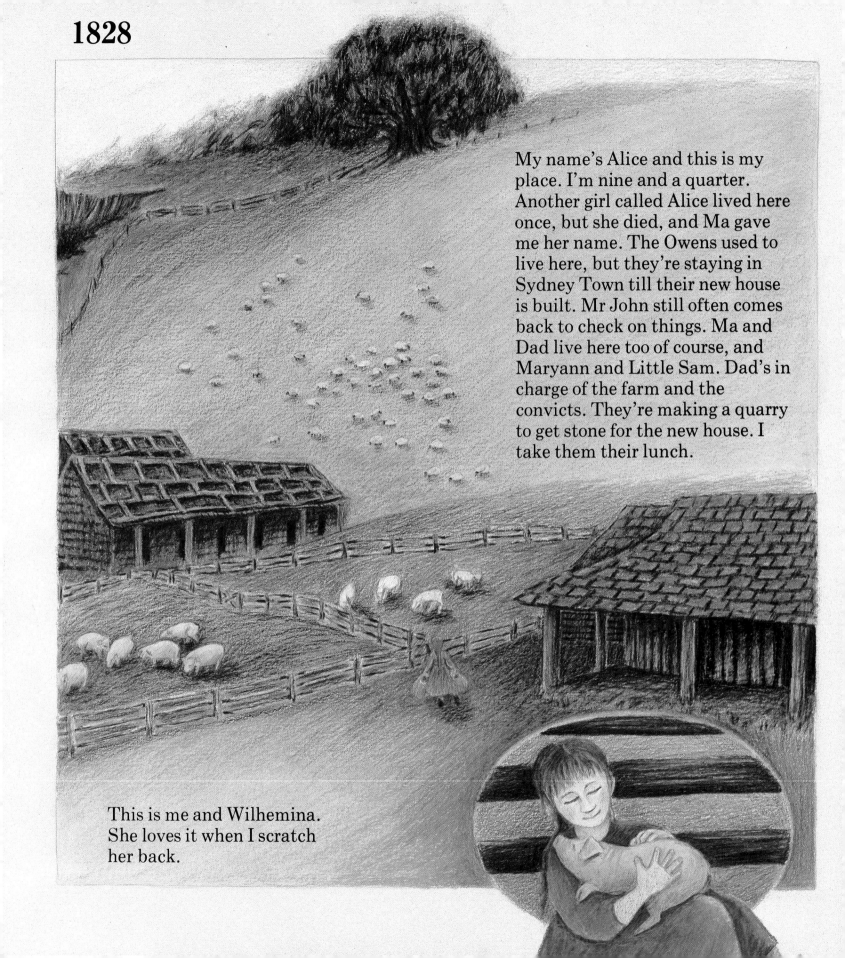

1828

My name's Alice and this is my place. I'm nine and a quarter. Another girl called Alice lived here once, but she died, and Ma gave me her name. The Owens used to live here, but they're staying in Sydney Town till their new house is built. Mr John still often comes back to check on things. Ma and Dad live here too of course, and Maryann and Little Sam. Dad's in charge of the farm and the convicts. They're making a quarry to get stone for the new house. I take them their lunch.

This is me and Wilhemina. She loves it when I scratch her back.

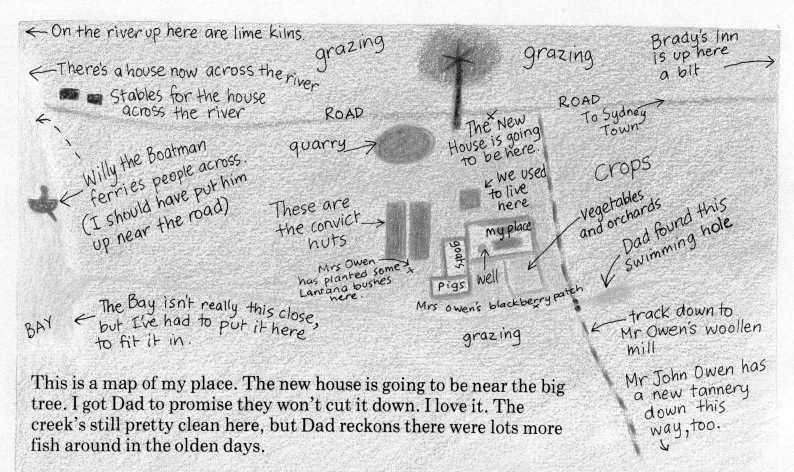

On the river up here are lime kilns.

grazing

grazing

Brady's Inn is up here a bit →

There's a house now across the river

Stables for the house across the river

ROAD

The New House is going to be here.

ROAD To Sydney Town

Willy the Boatman ferries people across. (I should have put him up near the road)

quarry →

we used to live here

Crops

These are the convict huts →

my place

Vegetables and orchards

Dad found this swimming hole

Mrs Owen has planted some Lantana bushes here.

goats

pigs   well

BAY   The Bay isn't really this close, but I've had to put it here to fit it in.

Mrs Owen's blackberry patch

grazing

track down to Mr Owen's woollen mill

Mr John Owen has a new tannery down this way, too.

This is a map of my place. The new house is going to be near the big tree. I got Dad to promise they won't cut it down. I love it. The creek's still pretty clean here, but Dad reckons there were lots more fish around in the olden days.

The night the Owens went, we all had a party. Dad used to be a convict too, so he doesn't treat the men like slaves, like Mr Owen and Mr John do. Ma roasted a whole sheep, and Old Freddie danced on the table.

1818

This is my place. My name's Charles and I'm eight and a half. I live here with my mother and my brother John and my sister Meg, and sometimes my father. I had another sister called Alice but she died. Sam and Sarah are our servants. Sam is in charge of things because Father is mostly in Sydney. John says Father is making money. He's got a new woollen mill across the swamp. John says he's going to make money too when he grows up, but I want to be a farmer.

This is me and Daisy. Sarah taught me to milk her. Sarah's nice. She lets me turn the handle on the butter-churn, and drink the buttermilk.

When Sam and Sarah got married, we had a party. Mother lent Sarah her second best shawl and Father gave them a guinea and three days' holiday. John got drunk on rum.

This is a map of my place. The long hut up the back is for the convicts. Mother says I'm not allowed to talk to them, but I do. The big tree is great to climb. When I'm up the top I pretend I've crossed the Blue Mountains, and I'm choosing some land for my very own farm. The other good thing is the creek. I build dams, but John breaks them up.

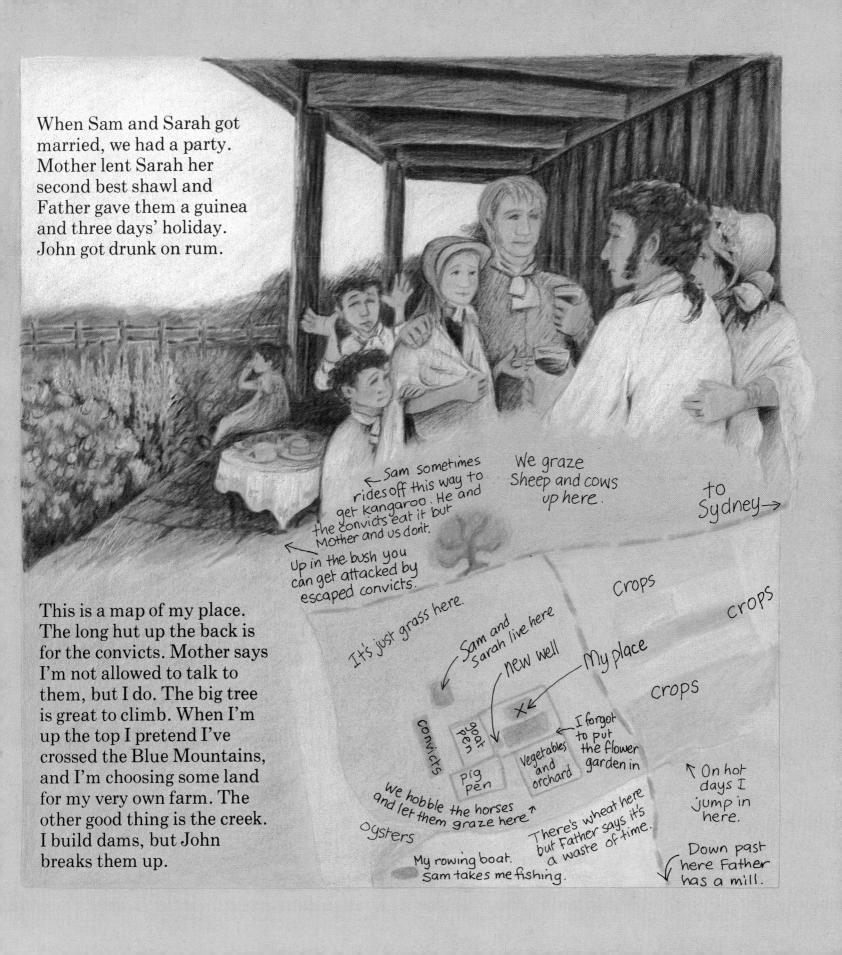

← Sam sometimes rides off this way to get kangaroo. He and the convicts eat it but Mother and us don't.

Up in the bush you can get attacked by escaped convicts.

We graze sheep and cows up here.

to Sydney →

It's just grass here.

Crops

crops

← Sam and Sarah live here

new well

My place

Convicts

goat pen

X

I forgot to put the flower garden in

pig pen

Vegetables and orchard

crops

We hobble the horses and let them graze here ↗

On hot days I jump in here.

Oysters

There's wheat here but Father says it's a waste of time.

My rowing boat. Sam takes me fishing.

Down past here Father has a mill.

1808

My name's Sarah and this is my place. I'm nine. I was born in Sydney but my mother came from England on a convict ship. Last year she died so Mrs Owen took me as a servant. She doesn't beat me much, but you should see all the work I have to do! Mrs Owen lives here too of course, and Alice and the baby John. Mr Owen's mainly in Sydney, doing business. Mrs Owen runs the farm, and she has five convict servants and Sam to help her. Sam used to be a convict but now he's a ticket-of-leave man. He's more like my family than anyone else in the world.

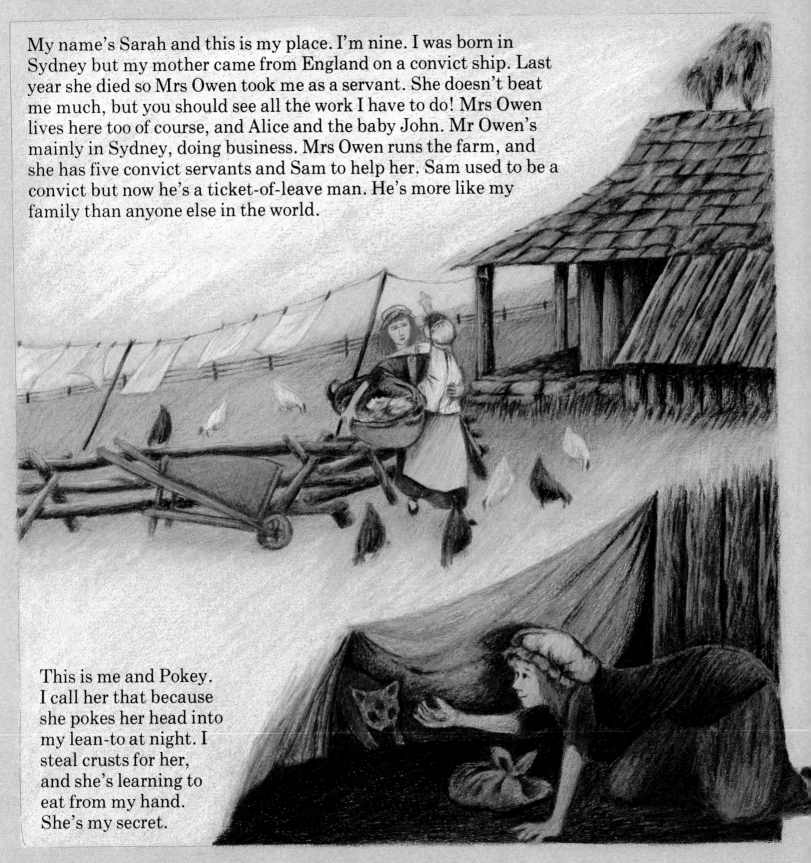

This is me and Pokey. I call her that because she pokes her head into my lean-to at night. I steal crusts for her, and she's learning to eat from my hand. She's my secret.

One day, some soldiers came to see Mr Owen. They ate and drank a lot, and talked about kicking out Governor Bligh. I hate it when adults get drunk and talk politics, so I nicked some jam roly and some oranges, and Alice and I went up to the big tree and had our own party.

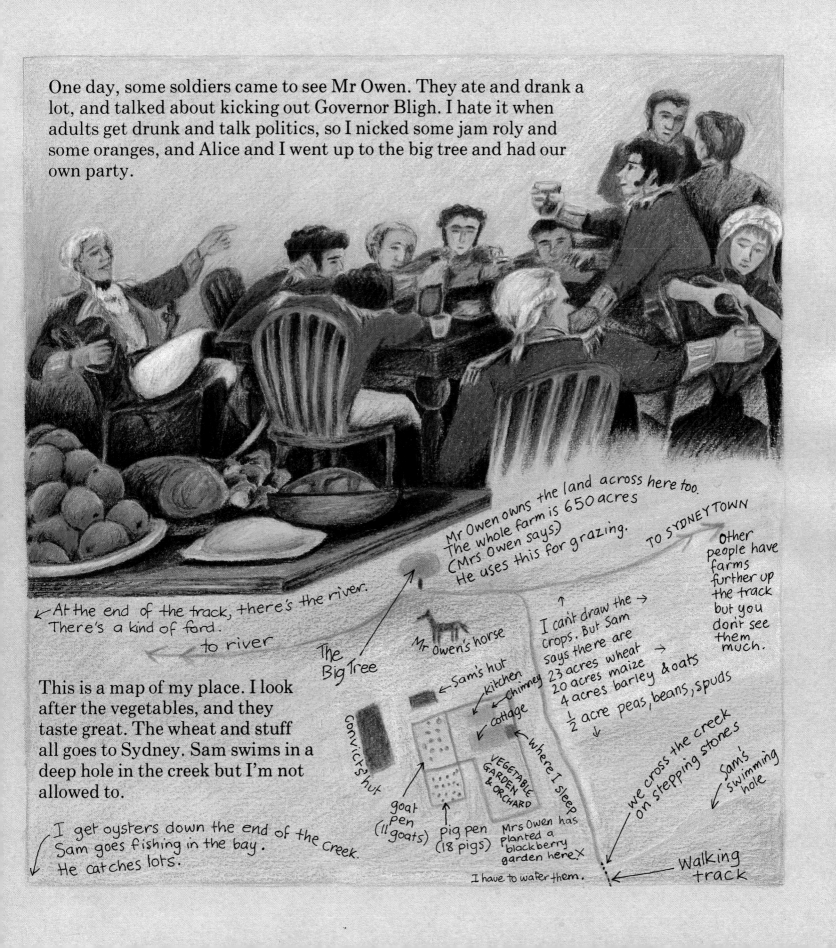

Mr Owen owns the land across here too. The whole farm is 650 acres (Mrs Owen says.) He uses this for grazing.

TO SYDNEY TOWN

Other people have farms further up the track but you don't see them much.

←At the end of the track, there's the river. There's a kind of ford.

to river

The Big Tree

Mr Owen's horse

I can't draw the → crops. But Sam says there are 23 acres wheat 20 acres maize 4 acres barley & oats ½ acre peas, beans, spuds

This is a map of my place. I look after the vegetables, and they taste great. The wheat and stuff all goes to Sydney. Sam swims in a deep hole in the creek but I'm not allowed to.

← Sam's hut
Kitchen
chimney
cottage
where I sleep

Convict's hut

we cross the creek on stepping stones

Sam's swimming hole

VEGETABLE GARDEN & ORCHARD

I get oysters down the end of the creek. Sam goes fishing in the bay. He catches lots.

goat pen (11 goats)

pig pen (18 pigs)

Mrs Owen has planted a blackberry garden here.X

I have to water them.

Walking track

1798

This is my place. My name's Sam, and I was born in London. I'm eleven. The judge put me in gaol because I stole a jacket. I was cold. In the gaol they beat me. Then they put me on a ship and sent me here. Then they let me out to work for Mr Owen. Sometimes he whips me too. But at least it's not cold, and I can catch heaps of fish to eat.

Last Christmas, Mr Owen gave me a holiday. Mrs Owen is still in England and she sent out a pudding. Mr Owen drank a lot of rum and let me eat as much as I liked. I've never had a pudding or a holiday before.

This is me and Katie. I milk her every morning, and at night I put her in the pen in case the blacks get her.

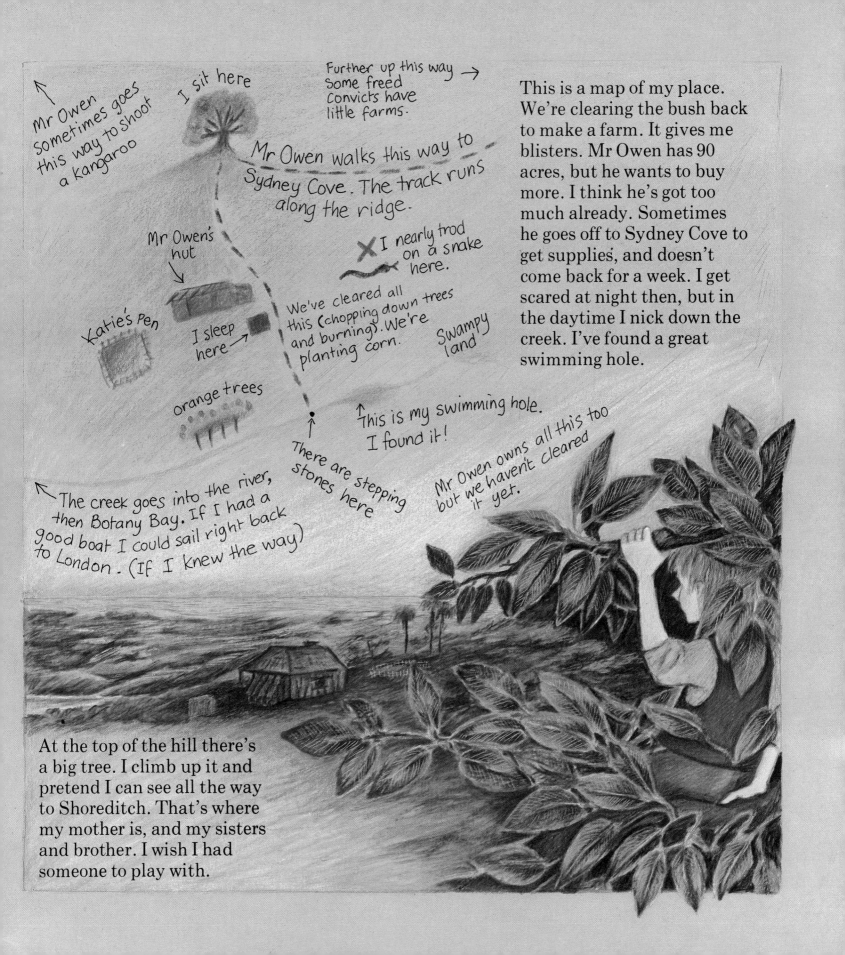

Mr Owen sometimes goes this way to shoot a kangaroo

I sit here

Further up this way some freed convicts have little farms.

Mr Owen walks this way to Sydney Cove. The track runs along the ridge.

Mr Owen's hut

I nearly trod on a snake here.

We've cleared all this (chopping down trees and burning). We're planting corn.

Swampy land

Katie's Pen

I sleep here →

orange trees

There are stepping stones here

This is my swimming hole. I found it!

Mr Owen owns all this too but we haven't cleared it yet.

The creek goes into the river, then Botany Bay. If I had a good boat I could sail right back to London. (If I knew the way)

This is a map of my place. We're clearing the bush back to make a farm. It gives me blisters. Mr Owen has 90 acres, but he wants to buy more. I think he's got too much already. Sometimes he goes off to Sydney Cove to get supplies, and doesn't come back for a week. I get scared at night then, but in the daytime I nick down the creek. I've found a great swimming hole.

At the top of the hill there's a big tree. I climb up it and pretend I can see all the way to Shoreditch. That's where my mother is, and my sisters and brother. I wish I had someone to play with.

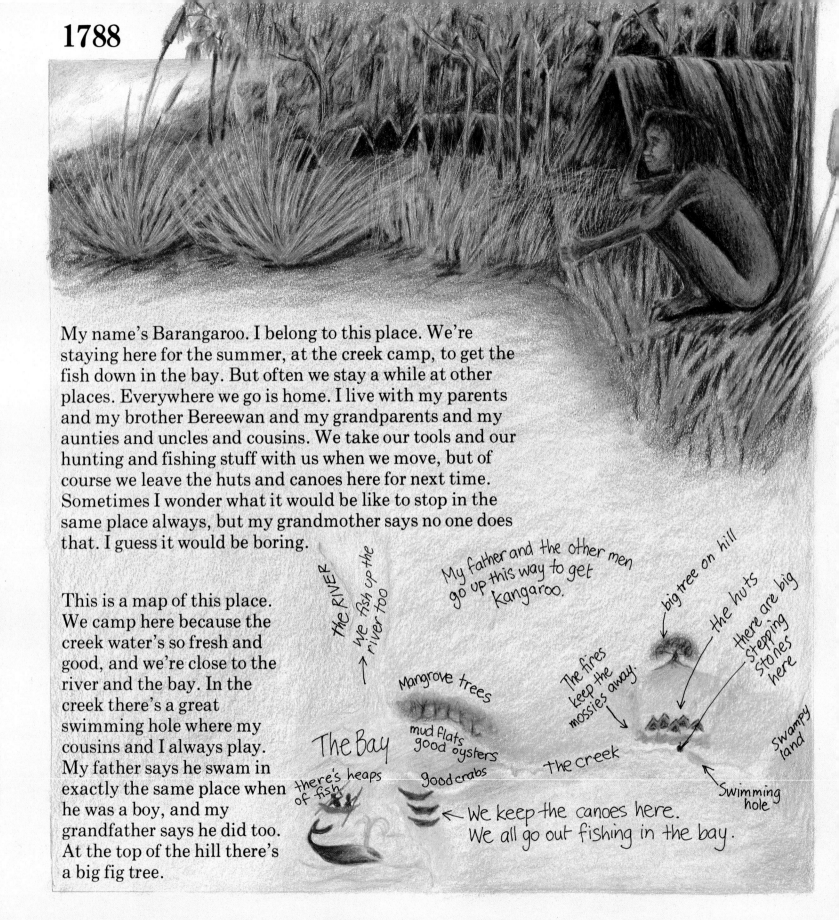

My name's Barangaroo. I belong to this place. We're staying here for the summer, at the creek camp, to get the fish down in the bay. But often we stay a while at other places. Everywhere we go is home. I live with my parents and my brother Bereewan and my grandparents and my aunties and uncles and cousins. We take our tools and our hunting and fishing stuff with us when we move, but of course we leave the huts and canoes here for next time. Sometimes I wonder what it would be like to stop in the same place always, but my grandmother says no one does that. I guess it would be boring.

This is a map of this place. We camp here because the creek water's so fresh and good, and we're close to the river and the bay. In the creek there's a great swimming hole where my cousins and I always play. My father says he swam in exactly the same place when he was a boy, and my grandfather says he did too. At the top of the hill there's a big fig tree.

The RIVER

We fish up the river too

My father and the other men go up this way to get kangaroo.

big tree on hill

the huts

there are big stepping stones here

The fires keep the mossies away.

Mangrove trees

mud flats good oysters

The Bay

there's heaps of fish

good crabs

the creek

Swampy land

Swimming hole

We keep the canoes here. We all go out fishing in the bay.

This is our dog. He sleeps with me.

Last week a whale got washed up on the bay, so we invited some other people from round about, and had a big barbecue. As well as the meat, we had piles of vegetables, and oysters and pippies and crabs and octopus and I've forgotten what else. I ate so much I thought I'd explode. Then I fell asleep till the night-time party started.

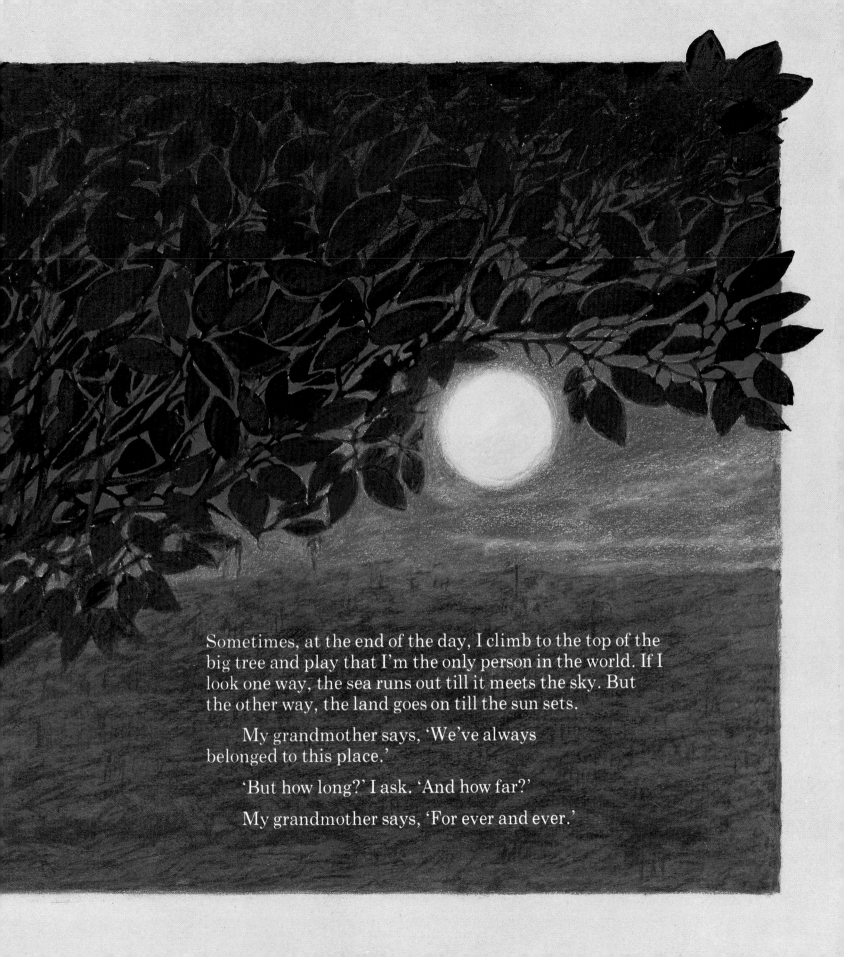

Sometimes, at the end of the day, I climb to the top of the
big tree and play that I'm the only person in the world. If I
look one way, the sea runs out till it meets the sky. But
the other way, the land goes on till the sun sets.

My grandmother says, 'We've always
belonged to this place.'

'But how long?' I ask. 'And how far?'

My grandmother says, 'For ever and ever.'

Acknowledgements

We'd like to thank all the people who
helped us do the research for this book,
especially Carol Allport, Chrys Meader,
Fred McCarthy and Annie Ross. Thanks
too to Collins Dove, for believing in us and our
ideas, and to Gay, for enthusiastic
typesetting. Finally, thanks to
David and Ken, for being sounding
boards and life support systems.